DICKENS LIBRARY

A Tale of Two Cities

by Charles Dickens

abridged edition

Published in Great Britain by World International Publishing Limited.
P.O. Box 111, Great Ducie Street, Manchester M60 3BL.
Printed in The G.D.R. SBN 7235 7658 0.

Book the First: Recalled to Life

The Period

It was the best of times, it was the worst of times; it was the age of wisdom, it was the age of foolishness; it was the spring of hope, it was the winter of despair; we had everything before us, we had nothing before us. It was the year one thousand seven hundred and seventy-five.

The Preparation

On a Friday night late in November, Mr Jarvis Lorry, of Tellson's Bank, London, arrived at Dover on the mail coach. He waited in the Royal George hotel for his guest, Miss Manette.

Miss Lucie Manette was a young lady of not more than seventeen, a short, slight figure with golden hair and blue eyes. As his eyes rested on her a vivid likeness passed before Mr Lorry of a child he had held in his arms on a passage across the Channel from France many years before.

"I received a letter from the Bank respecting the property of my poor father," said Miss Manette, "whom I never saw – so long dead. It said I should go to Paris with you, and that you would explain the details of the business."

Mr Lorry began the story of one of his customers. "He was a French gentleman, a doctor of Beauvais, who married an English lady."

"But this is my father's story," said Miss Manette, "and I think that when I was left an orphan by my mother's surviving my father only two years, it was you who brought me to England."

"It *was* I," said Mr Lorry. "You have been the ward of Tellson's since."

Then Mr Lorry continued. "So far," he said, "this is the story of your father. Now comes the difference. If he had not died; if he had suddenly and silently disappeared to the oblivion of a prison; if his wife had implored in vain for any tidings of him – then the history of your father would have been the history of this unfortunate gentleman. This doctor's wife had suffered so intensely before her child was born that she determined to rear her in the belief that her father was dead. Your mother took this course with you. But your father has been found. He is alive. He is with an old servant in Paris, and we are going there. But this is a secret. All is comprehended in the one line: 'Recalled to Life'."

The Wine Shop

In a wine shop in the suburb of Saint Antoine, Paris, sat Mr Lorry and Miss Manette.

Mr Lorry spoke to Monsieur Defarge, the owner. Their conference was very short, but very decided, and soon all three went out, leaving Madame Defarge knitting, seeing nothing.

Monsieur Defarge led the way to the top room of a house. The garret was dim and dark; inside a white-haired man sat on a low bench, making shoes.

The Shoemaker

"Good day!" said Monsieur Defarge. "You are hard at work?"

After a long silence the man's voice replied, "Yes – I am working."

The man had a white beard, raggedly cut, a hollow face, and exceedingly bright eyes. His shirt lay open and showed his body to be withered and worn.

"Tell your visitor what kind of shoe you make, and the maker's name," said Monsieur Defarge.

"It is a lady's shoe," said the man. "And my name? One Hundred and Five, North Tower." And with a weary sound that was not a sigh, nor a groan, he bent to work again.

Miss Manette moved and stood beside him.

"What is this?" he said and, advancing his hand little by little, he took up her golden hair and looked at it. Then he put his hand to his neck and took off a blackened string with a scrap of rag attached to it. It contained two long golden hairs. "It is the same," he said. "How can it be! She laid her head upon my shoulder that night when I was summoned, and in the North Tower I found the hairs upon my sleeve. How was this? Was it you? No, no – that was long ago. What is your name?"

His daughter fell upon her knees. "Oh, sir, at another time you shall know my name," she said. "But I cannot tell you at this time, here. Your agony is over; I have come to take you to England."

Mr Lorry and Monsieur Defarge made ready for the journey and the man, long accustomed to obey, boarded the coach.

Book the Second: The Golden Thread

Five Years Later

Tellson's Bank was an old-fashioned place, even in the year one thousand seven hundred and eighty. It was very small, very dark, and very ugly.

Outside Tellson's sat an odd-job-man, an occasional porter and messenger never absent during business hours, unless upon an errand, and then he was represented by his son: a grisly urchin of twelve, his express image. The man's name was Jerry Cruncher.

A Sight

One March morning Jerry was told to take a message to Mr Lorry at the Old Bailey courts, where a treason case was being tried.

At the Bailey, Jerry watched as the prisoner was brought in. He was a young man of about five-and-twenty, well-grown and well-looking. His condition was that of a young gentleman. He was plainly dressed and his hair, which was long and dark, was gathered in a ribbon.

Silence in the court! Charles Darnay had pleaded Not Guilty to an indictment denouncing him as a traitor to the King, by having assisted Lewis, the French King, in his wars against the said King, by wickedly, traitorously revealing what forces our King had ready to send to Canada and North America.

The accused was quiet and attentive, until he glimpsed two persons upon whom his look immediately rested, a young lady of little more than twenty, and a gentleman, evidently her father, a man of remarkable appearance in respect of the absolute whiteness of his hair and intensity of face. They were witnesses against the prisoner.

A Disappointment

Mr Attorney-General had to inform the jury that the prisoner, though young in years, was old in treasonable practices. That it was certain that the prisoner had been in the habit of passing between France and England on secret business of which he could give no honest account. That a person who was beyond reproach had ferreted out the nature of the prisoner's schemes. That this patriot would be produced. That he had been the prisoner's friend, but had caused the prisoner's servant to examine his master's drawers and pockets, and secrete his papers. That the prisoner had been furnished with lists of His

Majesty's forces, their disposition and preparation, and had conveyed such information to a hostile power. That the proof would go back five years. That the jury must positively find the prisoner guilty, and make an end of him.

When the Attorney-General ceased, the patriot appeared in the witness box, John Barsad by name. Having released his noble bosom of its burden, the wigged gentleman sitting not far from Mr Lorry begged to ask him a few questions.

Had he ever been a spy himself? No. What did he live upon? His property. Where was his property? He didn't precisely remember. Ever been in prison, debtor's prison? Yes. How many times? Two or three times. Not five or six? Perhaps. Ever borrow money from the prisoner? Yes. Ever pay him back? No. Sure he saw the prisoner with the lists? Certain. Had not procured them himself? No. No motives but motives of patriotism? None whatsoever.

The servant, Roger Cly, swore his way through the case at a great rate. He had taken service with the prisoner four years ago. He began to have suspicions of the prisoner, and to keep an eye upon him, soon afterwards. He had seen lists. He had seen the prisoner show these lists to French gentlemen in Calais. He had known the last witness seven or eight years; that was mere coincidence.

Mr Attorney-General called Mr Jarvis Lorry. "Mr Lorry, look upon the prisoner," he said. "Have you seen him before?"

"I have. I was returning from France and at Calais he came on board and made the voyage with me."

"Were you travelling alone?"

"No, with two companions. A gentleman and lady. They are here."

"Miss Manette!" the Attorney-General called. "Have you seen the prisoner before?"

"Yes, on the ship just referred to."

"Had you any conversation with the prisoner?"

"Yes, my Lord. He noticed that my father was much fatigued and was so good as to shelter him from the wind and weather."

"Had he come on board alone?"

"No, two French gentlemen were with him. They conferred until the last moment."

"Had any papers been handed about among them?"

"Some, but I don't know what papers."

"Now, to the prisoner's conversation, Miss Manette," the Attorney-General continued.

"The prisoner was open in his confidence with me. He told me that he was travelling on delicate business, which might get people into trouble. He said this business had taken him to France, and might take him backwards and forwards between England and France for a long time to come. He was kind and good. I hope," she added, bursting into tears.

Mr Attorney-General now called for Doctor Manette. "Have you ever seen the prisoner before?" he asked.

"Once, when he called at my lodgings some three years ago."

"Can you identify him as your fellow passenger on the boat?"

"Sir, I can do neither."

"Is there a special reason for your being unable to do so?"

"A long imprisonment," he answered.

"Have you no memory of the occasion?"

"None. My mind is a blank. I have no remembrance."

A singular circumstance then arose in the case. The object being to show that the prisoner had travelled to a garrison and dockyard and there collected information, a witness was called.

The witness was quite sure.

"Did you ever see anybody very like the prisoner?"

Not so like (the witness said) that he could be mistaken.

"Look well upon my learned friend there," he said, pointing to his colleague, Sydney Carton, "and then look upon the prisoner. Are they very like each other?"

Allowing for my learned friend's appearance being careless and slovenly, they were sufficiently like each other to surprise not only the witness, but everybody present.

Mr Stryver (the prisoner's counsel) asked the witness if what had happened once, might happen twice. The upshot of which was to smash this witness like a crockery pot.

Mr Stryver now addressed the jury, showing them how the patriot, Barsad, was a hired spy and traitor, one of the greatest scoundrels on earth. How the servant, Cly, was his friend and partner; how their watchful eyes had rested on the prisoner as a victim because some family affairs in France required his making those passages across the Channel, though what those affairs were he could not disclose.

And now the jury retired. Mr Lorry beckoned to Jerry Cruncher. "You will be here when the jury come in. I want you to take the verdict back to the bank."

An hour and a half limped heavily away and the messenger had dropped into a doze when a loud murmur woke him.

Mr Lorry handed him a paper. Hastily written on it was the word ACQUITTED.

Congratulatory

Doctor Manette, Lucie, Mr Lorry and Mr Stryver stood around Mr Charles Darnay – just released – congratulating him on his escape from death.

Mr Darnay kissed Lucie's hand fervently and gratefully,

and turned to Mr Stryver, whom he warmly thanked.

Lucie and her father departed in a carriage, and Mr Stryver made his way to the robing-room. Another person, who had been leaning against the wall where its shadow was blackest, now stepped up. Nobody had made any acknowledgement of Mr Carton's part in the day's proceedings; nobody had known of it.

Mr Lorry set off for Tellson's, and Carton turned to Darnay. "This is a strange chance that throws you and me together," he said. "This must be strange to you, standing alone with your counterpart."

He led Darnay to a little room in a tavern where Charles was soon recruiting his strength with dinner and wine.

"Do you feel that you belong to this terrestrial scheme again, Mr Darnay?" Carton asked.

"I am confused regarding time and place; but I am so far mended as to feel that."

"As to me, the greatest desire I have is to forget that I belong to it. It has no good in it for me – except wine like this – nor I for it. So we are not much alike in that particular. I think we are not much alike in any particular. Why don't you give a toast?"

"Miss Manette, then!"

"That's a fair young lady to be wept for by! Is it worth being tried for one's life to be the object of such evident sympathy and compassion, Mr Darnay?"

Darnay did not answer, but thanked Carton for his assistance.

"I neither want any thanks, nor merit any," was the careless rejoinder. "I don't know why I did it. Do you think I particularly like you?"

"You have acted as if you do; but I don't think you do."

"*I* don't think I do," said Carton.

Charles Darnay rose and wished him goodnight.

When he was alone Carton went to a glass on the wall.

"Do you particularly like the man?" he muttered at his own image. "Why should you like a man who resembles you? There is nothing in you to like. Change places with him, and would you have been looked at by those blue eyes as he was, and commiserated by that agitated face as he was? Come on, have it out in plain words! You hate the fellow."

Hundreds of People

On the afternoon of a certain fine Sunday Mr Jarvis Lorry walked along sunny streets to dine at the lodgings of Doctor Manette.

The Doctor and Miss Lucie were out, but expected home, and Mr Lorry waited inside, where he spoke to Miss Pross, a wild red woman who was Miss Lucie's companion. She was one of those unselfish creatures who will, for pure love, bind themselves willing slaves, to youth when they have lost it, to beauty they never had, to bright hopes that never shone upon their own lives.

"I am very much put out about my Ladybird," she said. "I don't want dozens of people who are not at all worthy of her to come here looking for her."

"*Do* dozens come?" asked Mr Lorry.

"Hundreds," said Miss Pross.

Soon Doctor Manette and Lucie returned, but no Hundreds of People came to see the sights.

Dinner time, and still no Hundreds of People.

After dinner, Lucie proposed that they should sit outside. Mr Darnay presented himself as they sat, but he was the only one. Doctor Manette received him kindly, and so did Lucie. But Miss Pross suddenly became afflicted with a twitching in the head and body, and retired to the house.

"Have you seen much of the Tower, Doctor?" asked Mr Darnay. "*I* have been there, as you remember, and they told me a curious thing. In making alterations workmen came upon an old dungeon. Every stone of its wall was covered by inscriptions carved by prisoners – dates, names, prayers. Upon a corner stone were three letters: D I G. There had been no prisoner with these initials, and it was suggested that the letters were the complete word, DIG. Under a stone in the floor were found the ashes of a paper, mingled with the ashes of a small leather bag. What the unknown prisoner had written will never be read."

Doctor Manette suddenly started up, with his hand to his head. His manner and look terrified them all. "There are large drops of rain falling, and they made me start," he said. "We had better go in."

He recovered himself almost instantly, and said not a word about the discovery that he had been told of.

Tea-time, and Miss Pross making tea, with another fit of the jerks, yet no Hundreds of People. Mr Carton had arrived, but he made only two.

They all moved to one of the windows and looked out into the heavy twilight.

There was a great hurry of people in the streets, speeding away to shelter before the storm broke; the house resounded with the echoes of footsteps.

"There is a great crowd coming into our lives," said Sydney Carton. "Are they to come to all of us, or are we to divide them among us?"

"I have imagined them the footsteps of the people who are to come into my life, and my father's."

"I hear them!" said Carton, after a peal of thunder and a vivid flash of lightning. "Here they come, fast, fierce and furious!"

It was one in the morning when Mr Lorry, Mr Darnay and Mr Carton made their way home together. "Goodnight," said Mr Lorry. "Shall we ever see such a night again, together!"

Perhaps. Perhaps, see the great crowd of people bearing down upon them, too.

Monseigneur in Town

Monseigneur, one of the great lords at the Court, held his reception in his grand hotel in Paris.

Monseigneur had one truly noble idea of general public business, which was to let everything go on in its own way. Monseigneur had the other truly noble idea that it must all go his way – tend to his own power and pocket. Of his pleasures, Monseigneur had the other truly noble idea that the world was made for them.

In his rooms were military officers, destitute of military knowledge; naval officers with no idea of a ship; brazen ecclesiastics; all totally unfit for their callings, all lying horribly in pretending to belong to them.

Bestowing a word here and a smile there Monseigneur passed through them, the show being over, there was one person left, who passed among the mirrors on his way out. "I demote you," said this person, "to the Devil!"

He was about sixty, handsomely dressed, haughty in manner, with a face like a fine mask.

He got into his carriage and drove away with a wild rattle and clatter, the common people dispersing before his horses, barely escaping being run down. At last, swooping at a corner, one of the wheels came to a jolt and the horses reared and plunged.

"What has gone wrong?" said Monsieur.

"Pardon, Monsieur the Marquis!" said a ragged man. "It is a child."

A tall man bent over the tiny bundle. "Killed!" he shrieked. "Dead!"

The people closed round and looked at the Marquis. He threw out a gold coin. "It is extraordinary," he said, "that you cannot take care of your children. How do I know what injury you have done to my horses?"

The tall man called out again, "Dead!"

He was stopped by the arrival of Monsieur Defarge, who spoke to him. "Be a brave man, my Gaspard!" he said. "It is better for the poor thing to die so, than to live. Could it have lived an hour as happily?"

"Pick up that, philosopher," said the Marquis, throwing another coin.

He was being driven away when a coin flew into his carriage. "Hold!" he said. "Who threw that? If I knew which rascal threw, and if that brigand were sufficiently near it, he should be crushed under the wheels."

Not a voice, or a hand, or even an eye was raised, and the Marquis drove on.

Monseigneur in the Country

At the top of a steep hill the Marquis's carriage halted for an adjustment to be made to the wheels, then travelled on to a poor village, where the Marquis pointed out one of the peasants. "I passed you on the hill?" he asked.

"I had the honour of being passed on the road," said the road mender.

"What did you look at so fixedly?"

"I looked at the man," he said, pointing under the carriage. "He swung there by a chain."

"Who was he?"

"I never saw him before. He was whiter than the miller, all covered with dust, tall as a spectre!"

"Did he run away, when we stopped?"

"He went over the hill-side head first."

"Bah!" said the Marquis. "Drive on!"

At the great door of his chateau he stopped. "Monsieur Charles, whom I expect; is he arrived from England?"

"Not yet."

A little later the nephew arrived. He had been known in England as Charles Darnay.

"You have been a long time coming," said the Marquis.

"I have been detained by – various business. I have come back, sir, pursuing the object that took me away. It carried me into great and unexpected peril; but it is a sacred object, and if it had carried me to death I hope it would have sustained me."

"Not to death," said the uncle.

"I believe it to be your bad fortune, and my good fortune, that has kept me out of prison here. I believe that if you were not in disgrace with the Court, a letter would have sent me to some fortress indefinitely."

"It is possible," said the uncle, "for the honour of the family."

"I believe our name to be detested more than any name in France."

"A compliment," said the Marquis, "to the grandeur of the family. The dark deference of fear and slavery will keep the dogs obedient to the whip."

"We have done wrong," said the nephew, "and are reaping the fruits of wrong."

"*We* have done wrong?"

"Our family; whose honour is of so much account to both of us, in such different ways. Even in my father's time we did a world of wrong. Can I separate my father's twin brother, inheritor and successor, from himself?"

"Death has done that!" said the Marquis.

"And has left me," answered the nephew, "bound to a system that is frightful to me, but powerless in it; seeking to execute the last request of my dear mother, which implored me to have mercy and redress."

"Seeking them from me," said the Marquis, "you will forever seek them in vain. I will die perpetuating the system under which I have lived. And you," he added, "how do you, under your new philosophy, intend to live?"

"I must do what others of my countrymen may have to do some day – work. In England. The family honour is safe from me in this country. The family name can suffer from me in no other, for I bear it in no other."

"England is the refuge of many. Do you know a doctor and his daughter who have found refuge there?"

"Yes."

"Yes," repeated the Marquis. "So commences the new philosophy! Goodnight. Light my nephew to his chamber, there! And burn him in his bed," he added to himself.

Next morning the chateau woke gradually and surely. But why did the great bell ring? Why did figures run here and there, and horses ride away?

It portended that there was one stone face too many at the chateau. It lay back on the pillow of Monsieur the Marquis. It was like a fine mask. Driven home into the heart of the figure was a knife. Round its hilt was a paper on which was scrawled: *"Drive him fast to his tomb. This, from JACQUES".*

Two Promises

Twelve months had come and gone, and Mr Charles Darnay was established in England as a teacher of French. With great perseverance and untiring industry, he prospered. He had expected labour and he found it, and did it, and made the best of it.

He had loved Lucie Manette from the hour of his danger. He had never heard a sound so dear as the sound of her compassionate voice; had never seen a face so beautiful as hers.

One day he determined to open his mind to Doctor Manette when he knew Lucie to be out with Miss Pross.

He found the doctor reading at a window. "Dear Doctor Manette, I love your daughter," he said, "fondly, dearly, devotedly. If ever there were love in the world, I love her."

"I do not doubt your loving Lucie," said the doctor. "Have you spoken to Lucie?"

"No."

"Have you any reason to believe that Lucie loves you?"

"None. As yet, none."

"I give a promise," said the doctor. "If she should ever tell me that you are essential to her perfect happiness, I will give her to you."

"Your confidence in me ought to be returned with full confidence on my part," said Darnay. "My present name is not my own. I wish to tell you what that is, and why I am in England."

"Stop!" said the doctor of Beauvais. "Tell me when I ask you, not now. If Lucie should love you, tell me on your marriage morning. Do you promise?"

"Willingly."

The Fellow of No Delicacy

If Sydney Carton shone anywhere, he certainly never shone in the house of Doctor Manette. He had been there often, and had always been the same moody and morose lounger there.

And yet he did care something for the streets that environed that house. Many a night he vaguely wandered there; many a dreary daybreak revealed his solitary figure lingering there.

One day in August he went to the doctor's house and found Lucie alone. She had never been quite at ease with him, and received him with some little embarrassment. "I fear you are not well, Mr Carton!" she observed.

"The life I lead is not conducive to health."

"Is it not a pity to live no better life?" asked Lucie, who was surprised to see that there were tears in his eyes.

"It is too late for that. I shall never be better than I am. I shall sink lower, and be worse. Pray forgive me. I break down before the knowledge of what I want to say to you. If it had been possible that you could have returned the love of the man you see before you – wasted, drunken creature as you know him to be – he would have been conscious, in spite of his happiness, that he would bring you to misery, blight you, disgrace you. I wish you to know that you have been the last dream of my soul. Since I knew you I have been troubled by a remorse that I thought would never reproach me again. I distress you; I draw fast to an end. Will you let me believe that the last confidence of my life lies in your innocent breast, and will be shared by no one?"

"Mr Carton," Lucie answered, "the secret is yours, not mine; and I promise to respect it."

He put her hand to his lips, and moved towards the door. "In the hour of my death I shall hold sacred that my last avowal of myself was made to you, and that my name, and faults, and miseries were gently carried in your heart."

He was so unlike what he had ever shown himself to be, and it was so sad to think how much he had thrown away, that Lucie wept for him.

"Be comforted!" he said. "I am not worth such feeling. Within myself I shall always be what I am now, though outwardly I shall be what you have seen before. For you, and for any dear to you, I would do anything. The time will not be long in coming when new ties will be formed about you – the dearest ties that will grace and gladden you. Oh, Miss Manette, think now and then that there is a man who would give his life, to keep a life you love beside you!"

The Honest Tradesman

One day Jerry Cruncher observed a funeral. "Who is it?" he asked.

"Spy!" said a spectator. "Old Bailey spy! Roger Cly."

"Why, to be sure!" exclaimed Jerry, recalling the trial he had witnessed. "I've seen him."

The large crowd that had gathered jeered and shouted, and the coach doors were opened. The one mourner scuffled out and in a moment was away up a by-street.

The dead man disposed of, the crowd eventually dispersed, their sport over; Mr Cruncher remained behind to confer with the undertakers.

That night Jerry said that he was going fishing, and at one o'clock he opened a locked cupboard and brought forth a sack, a crowbar, a rope and chain, and other fishing tackle of that nature.

Young Jerry, his son, had been ordered to bed, but was not long after his father, who soon collected two other fishermen.

The three scaled an iron gate, then moved away on their hands and knees. They were in a churchyard.

They fished with a spade first, then there was a screwing and complaining sound down below and the figures were strained, as if by a weight. By slow degrees the weight came to the surface. Young Jerry knew what it would be, but when he saw it, he was so frightened that he ran all the way home.

There was no fish for breakfast, but Mr Cruncher was washed and brushed at the usual hour, and set off with his son for Tellson's.

Young Jerry, his cunning now fresh with the day, asked, "Father, what's a Resurrection-Man?"

"Well," returned Mr Cruncher, "he's a tradesman."

"What's the goods?"

"His goods is a branch of scientific goods."

"Persons' bodies, ain't it?" asked Young Jerry. "I should like to be a Resurrection-Man when I'm quite growed up!"

Knitting

There had been earlier drinking than usual in the wine-shop of Monsieur Defarge, though the master was not visible.

It was high noontide when two dusty men entered: one was Monsieur Defarge, the other a mender of roads.

The man was taken outside, up a steep staircase into a garret – the garret where a white-haired man had sat on a bench, making shoes.

Defarge closed the door, and spoke to three other men who had gathered there. "Jacques One, Jacques Two, Jacques Three! This is the witness encountered by me, Jacques Four. He will tell you all. Speak, Jacques Five!"

"I saw him," began the mender of roads, "a year ago, underneath the carriage of the Marquis, hanging by the chain. This tall man is lost – and he is sought ten, eleven months when I see him again with six soldiers. I follow. They bring him up to the prison. In the morning I see him, high up, behind the bars of a lofty iron cage; he regards me like a dead man."

Defarge and the three glanced darkly at one another.

"He remains there for some days. They whisper that he will not be executed; petitions have been presented to the King himself. Again they whisper that he will be executed. On Monday morning there is raised a gallows. He is hanged there – and is left hanging. I left at sunset and walked until I met this comrade."

"How say you?" demanded Number One. "To be registered?"

"To be registered as doomed to destruction," returned

Defarge. "The chateau and all the race. Extermination."

"Are you sure that the register is safe? Shall we always be able to decipher it – or will she?"

"Knitted in her own stitches and her own symbols it will always be as plain to her as the sun. Confide in Madame Defarge."

"Is this rustic to be sent back soon?" asked another.

"He knows nothing," said Defarge. "He wishes to see the King, the Queen and Court; let him see them on Sunday."

"What?" exclaimed the man.

"Show a cat milk if you wish her to thirst for it," said Defarge. "Show a dog his natural prey if you wish him to bring it down one day."

Still Knitting

The road mender returned to his village and Madame Defarge and her husband to the wine-shop. "There is another spy in our quarter," said Defarge. "John Barsad. Age, about forty years; height, about five feet nine; black hair, complexion dark; nose not straight."

"He shall be registered tomorrow," said Madame.

Next noontide saw her knitting when a stranger entered. "Good day," she said, but added to herself: "About forty, black hair. JOHN BARSAD."

"A bad business, Gaspard's execution," said Barsad.

"If people use knives, they have to pay," returned Madame. "He has paid the price."

Barsad turned to Monsieur Defarge. "I know of some interesting connections with your name," he said. "When Doctor Manette was released, you, his old domestic, had the charge of him. It was to you that his daughter came. I have known them, in England. Miss Manette is going to be married – to the nephew of the Marquis; in other words, the present Marquis. He lives unknown in England; he is Mr Charles Darnay. D'Aulnais is the name of his mother's family."

Madame Defarge knitted steadily, but the intelligence had a palpable effect on her husband, and the spy saw it.

When Barsad had left, Defarge turned to his wife. "Can it be true? Her husband's name is on the register?"

Nine Days

On Lucie's marriage-day she, Miss Pross and Mr Lorry waited outside the Doctor's room where he was speaking with Charles Darnay. When the Doctor appeared he was deadly pale.

Charles and Lucie were married, and set off for the country, but when Mr Lorry returned to visit the Doctor he was stopped by a low sound of knocking.

"All is lost!" said Miss Pross. "He doesn't know me, and is making shoes!"

Mr Lorry went into the Doctor's room. The shoemaker was very busy, but would not speak. He worked, and worked, and words fell on him as they would have fallen on the air.

The time went very slowly, and Mr Lorry's hope darkened, and his heart grew heavier every day, six days, seven days, eight days, nine days.

An Opinion

On the tenth morning Mr Lorry found the tools out aside, and the Doctor reading. He supposed that Lucie's wedding had taken place yesterday.

"My dear Manette," said Mr Lorry, "I am anxious to have your opinion on a very curious case, the case of an old and a prolonged shock. A shock from which he has recovered. But unfortunately there has been a slight relapse."

The Doctor asked, "Of how long?"

"Nine days and nights."

"Does his daughter know of the relapse?"

"No," replied Mr Lorry. "How does this relapse come about?"

"I believe," returned Doctor Manette, "that there had been a strong revival of the remembrance that was the first cause of the malady."

"As to the future," hinted Mr Lorry.

"As to the future, I should hope that the worst is over."

On the three following days the Doctor remained well, and on the fourteenth day he went to join Lucie and her husband for the rest of their holiday.

A Plea

When the newly-married pair came home, Sydney Carton spoke to Darnay. "You remember a certain occasion when I was more drunk then usual?" he said. "I was insufferable about liking you and not liking you. I wish you would forget it."

"I forgot it long ago," Darnay replied. "Have I had nothing more important to remember? The great service you rendered me that day?"

"Well, if you could endure to have a worthless fellow coming and going, I ask that I be permitted to come and go as a privileged person here."

Darnay agreed, and when Sydney had gone, made some mention of the conversation, and spoke of Sydney as a problem of carelessness and recklessness.

Later Lucie spoke to him. "I think poor Mr Carton deserves more consideration and respect," she said. "Be very generous with him always. He has a heart he very seldom reveals, and there are deep wounds in it. I have seen it bleeding. I am sure that he is capable of good things, even magnanimous things."

Echoing Footsteps

Some years passed. Darnay was prosperous, and Lucie the happy mother of a daughter of six.

On a night in mid-July, 1789, Mr Lorry came late from Tellson's. "There is such uneasiness in Paris," he said. "Our customers over there cannot confide their property to us fast enough. There is a mania for sending it to England."

Saint Antoine had been, that morning, a vast mass of scarecrows with gleams of light above the heads, where steel blades and bayonets shone in the sun.

"Come!" cried Defarge. "Patriots and friends, we are ready! The Bastille!"

With a roar that sounded as if all the breath in France had been shaped into the detested word, a living sea rose and overflowed the city to that point.

The attack began. Deep ditches, double drawbridge, massive stone walls, cannon, muskets, fire and smoke. Flashing weapons, blazing torches, bravery without stint, the furious sound of the living sea. Then a white flag from the fortress – suddenly the sea was over the drawbridge, past the stone walls. The Bastille surrendered!

"The prisoners!" was the cry taken up by the sea that rushed in, and Defarge went to the North Tower, to One Hundred and Five.

There was a small unglazed window high in the wall so that the sky could only be seen by stooping low and looking up. There was a stool, a table, a straw bed and four blackened walls. A.M. was scratched on one. "Alexandre Manette," said Defarge.

They searched the cell, found nothing, and left the tower.

Fire Rises

There was a change in the village where the mender of roads went forth daily. Far and wide lay a ruined country. Every green leaf, every blade of grass and blade of grain was as shrivelled and poor as the miserable people.

As the mender of roads worked he viewed a figure approaching on foot, a shaggy haired man, tall, in wooden shoes, steeped in the mud and dust of many highways.

"How goes it, Jacques?" the man said.

"Ah, well, Jacques."

They joined hands.

"Tonight?" said the mender of roads.

"Tonight," said the man.

That night, when the village had taken its poor supper, it did not creep to bed, but came out of doors again. A curious whispering was upon it, and all looked expectantly at the sky in one direction only.

The night deepened. The trees around the old chateau moved in a rising wind. Uneasy rushes went through the hall, and shook the curtain of the bed where the last Marquis had slept.

Presently the chateau began to make itself visible by some light of its own. Soon flames burst forth, and soared higher.

The chateau was left to itself to flame and burn, and four figures trudged away to their next destination.

In such risings of fire three years of tempest were consumed. Three more birthdays of little Lucie had been woven into the peaceful tissue of the life of her home.

Monseigneur, as a class, took to his noble heels.

The August of the year one thousand seven hundred and ninety-two was come, and Monseigneur was by this time scattered far and wide.

The great gathering-place of Monseigneur, in London, was Tellson's Bank.

On a steaming, misty afternoon, Mr Lorry sat at his desk, and Charles Darnay stood leaning on it, talking with him in a low voice.

"Although you are the youngest man that ever lived," said Charles, "I must still suggest."

"That I am too old?" said Mr Lorry.

"A long journey, a disorganised country, a city that may not be even safe for you."

"My dear Charles," said Mr Lorry, "it is safe enough for me. If I were not prepared to submit myself to a few inconveniences for the sake of Tellson's, who ought to be?"

A clerk approached Mr Lorry, and laying a soiled and unopened letter before him, asked if he had yet discovered any traces of the person to whom it was addressed? Darnay saw his own right name. The address, turned into English, ran: "Very pressing. To Monsieur heretofore the Marquis St Evrémonde, of France. Confided to the cares of Messrs Tellson and Co., Bankers, London, England."

Dr Manette had made it his one urgent request that the secret of this name should be kept between them. Nobody else knew it to be his name.

"No," said Mr Lorry, in reply to the clerk.

Darnay said, "I know the fellow."

"Will you take charge of the letter?" said Mr Lorry. "You know where to deliver it?"

"I do. I will come back to see you off."

Very ill at ease with himself, Darnay opened the letter, and read it:

Prison of the Abbaye, Paris
June 21, 1792

MONSIEUR HERETOFORE THE MARQUIS,

After having long been in danger of my life at the hands of

the village, I have been seized, and brought a long journey on foot to Paris. On the road I have suffered a great deal.

The crime for which I am imprisoned, and for which I shall lose my life is, treason against the majesty of the people, in that I have acted against them for an emigrant. It is in vain I represent that I have acted for them, and not against, according to your commands. It is in vain that I had collected no rent. The only response is, where is that emigrant? I cry in my sleep where is he? I demand of Heaven, will he not come to deliver me?

GABELLE.

The uneasiness in Darnay's mind was roused to life by this letter. The peril of an old servant whose only crime was fidelity to his family, stared him reproachfully in the face. He must go to Paris.

Neither Lucie nor her father must know of it until he was gone.

He walked until it was time to return to Tellson's and take leave of Mr Lorry. As soon as he arrived in Paris he would present himself to this old friend, but he must say nothing of his intention now.

"I have delivered that letter," said Charles Darnay. "I would not consent to your being charged with any written answer, but perhaps you will take a verbal one? It is to a prisoner in the Abbaye, Gabelle."

"Gabelle. And what is the message?"

"Simply, that he has received the letter, and will come. He will start upon his journey tomorrow night."

Book the Third: The Track of a Storm

In Secret

The traveller fared slowly who fared towards Paris from

England in the autumn of the year one thousand seven hundred and ninety-two. Every town-gate had its band of citizen-patriots, who stopped all comers and goers, inspected their papers, turned them back, or sent them on.

Darnay had been days upon his journey when he was awakened at the small inn to which he had been remitted until morning, in the middle of the night. Awakened by a timid local functionary and three armed patriots.

"Emigrant," said the functionary, "I am going to send you on to Paris, under an escort."

The escort were two mounted patriots in red caps who rode one on either side of him. When they came to the town of Beauvais the aspect of affairs was very alarming. An ominous crowd gathered to see him dismount and voices called out, "Down with the emigrant! He is a traitor since the decree. His life is forfeit to the people. His cursed life is not his own!"

Daylight found them before the wall of Paris. The barrier was closed and strongly guarded.

"Where are the papers of this prisoner?" demanded a resolute-looking man.

The patriot produced them. Casting his eyes over Gabelle's letter, the same personage in authority left without saying a word, and went into the guard-room.

After a half-hour, the man in authority directed the guard to open the barrier. The two patriots turned and rode away.

Darnay accompanied his conductor into a guard-room, where certain soldiers and patriots, asleep and awake, drunk and sober, were standing and lying about. Some registers were lying open on a desk, and an officer of a coarse, dark aspect, presided over these.

"Citizen Defarge," said he to Darnay's conductor. "Is this the emigrant Evrémonde?"

"This is the man."

"You are consigned, Evrémonde, to the prison of La

Force."

"Just Heaven!" exclaimed Darnay. "Under what law, and for what offence?"

"We have new laws, Evrémonde, and new offences, since you were here." He said it with a hard smile.

"Is it you," said Defarge, in a low voice, as they went down the guard-house steps, "who married the daughter of Doctor Manette, once a prisoner in the Bastille?"

"Yes," replied Darnay, looking at him with surprise.

"My name is Defarge, and I keep a wine-shop."

"My wife came to your house to reclaim her father? Yes!"

"In the name of that sharp female newly born, and called La Guillotine, why did you come to France?"

"Will you render me a little help?"

"None." Defarge spoke.

"Will you answer me a single question?"

"Perhaps."

"In this prison that I am going to so unjustly, shall I have some free communication with the world outside?"

"You will see."

"I am not to be buried there, prejudged?"

"You will see. Other people have been similarly buried in worse prisons, before now."

"But never by me, Citizen Defarge."

The prison of La Force was a gloomy prison, dark and filthy.

"Come!" said the gaoler, taking up his keys. "Come with me, emigrant."

Through the dismal prison twilight, his new charge accompanied him, many doors clanging and locking behind them, until they came to a large, low, vaulted chamber, crowded with prisoners.

Charles Darnay crossed to a grated door which closed under the gaoler's hand.

The wicket opened on a stone staircase, leading upward. When they had ascended forty steps the gaoler opened a low black door, and they passed into a solitary cell. It struck cold and damp, but was not dark.

"Yours," said the gaoler, and went out.

"Five paces by four and a half, five paces by four and a half." The prisoner walked to and fro in his cell, counting its measurement. "He made shoes, he made shoes, he made shoes."

The Grindstone

Tellson's Bank in Paris was in a wing of a large house, approached by a court-yard and shut off from the street by a high wall and a strong gate.

Mr Jarvis Lorry sat by a fire and on his honest and courageous face there was a shade of horror.

On the opposite side of the court-yard was a large grindstone, which appeared to have hurriedly been brought there.

From the streets beyond the high wall and the strong gate, there came the usual night hum of the city, with now and then an indescribable ring in it, weird and unearthly.

"Thank God," said Mr Lorry, clasping his hands, "that no one near and dear to me is in this dreadful town tonight!" His door suddenly opened, and two figures rushed in, at sight of which he fell back in amazement.

Lucie and her father!

"What is this?" cried Mr Lorry, breathless and confused. "Lucie! Manette! What has happened?"

"Charles. Here."

"Here, in Paris?"

"Has been here some days – three or four – I don't know how many. An errand of generosity brought him here unknown to us; he was stopped and sent to prison."

The old man uttered an irrepressible cry. Almost at the same moment, a loud noise of feet and voices came pouring into the court-yard.

"What is that noise?" said the Doctor.

"Don't look!" cried Mr Lorry.

The Doctor turned, and said, with a cool bold smile: "My dear friend, I have a charmed life in this city. I have been a Bastille prisoner. There is no patriot in France, who, knowing me to have been a prisoner in the Bastille, would touch me, except to overwhelm me with embraces. My old pain has given me a power that has gained us news of Charles and brought us here."

"What prison is he in?" said Mr Lorry.

"La Force!"

"La Force! Lucie, my child, you cannot possibly stir out. You must be obedient, still, and quiet. You must let me put you in a room at the back here. You must leave your father and me alone."

"I will be submissive to you. I know you are true."

The old man came hurrying back to the Doctor, and looked out with him into the court-yard. Looked out upon a throng of men and women: forty or fifty in all. They had rushed in to work at the grindstone; it had evidently been set up there for their purpose.

But, such awful workers, and such awful work! Hatchets, knives, swords, all brought to be sharpened.

"They are," Mr Lorry whispered, "murdering the prisoners. If you really have the power you think you have – make yourself known to these devils, and get taken to La Force. It may be too late, I don't know, but let it not be a minute later!"

Doctor Manette hastened out of the room.

His streaming white hair, his remarkable face, and the confidence of his manner, carried him in an instant to the heart of the concourse at the stone.

The Shadow

Mr Lorry removed Lucie, her child and Miss Pross to a lodging, and left Jerry with them.

He was again alone in his room when he heard a foot upon the stair. In a few moments, a man stood in his presence, who addressed him by his name.

"I have seen you somewhere," said Mr Lorry.

"Perhaps at my wine-shop?"

Mr Lorry said: "You come from Doctor Manette? What does he send me?"

Defarge gave him a scrap of paper: *Charles is safe, but I cannot safely leave this place yet. The bearer has a short note from Charles to his wife. Let the bearer see his wife.*

"Will you accompany me," said Mr Lorry, "to where his wife resides?"

"Yes," returned Defarge. They went down into the court-yard. There, they found two women; one, knitting.

"Madame Defarge, surely!" said Mr Lorry. "Does Madame go with us?"

"Yes. That she may be able to recognise the persons. It is for their safety."

They were admitted by Jerry, and found Lucie weeping. She read the note: *Dearest, Take courage. I am well, and your father has influence around me. You cannot answer this. Kiss our child for me.*

"Is that his child?" said Madame Defarge, stopping in her work and pointing her knitting-needle at little Lucie as if it were the finger of Fate.

"Yes, madame," answered Mr Lorry.

The shadow attendant on Madame Defarge seemed to fall, threatening and dark, on the mother and child.

"It is enough, my husband," said Madame Defarge. "I have seen them. We may go."

Calm in Storm

Doctor Manette did not return until the morning of the fourth day of his absence.

The crowd had taken him through a scene of carnage to the prison of La Force, where he had found a Tribunal sitting. He had announced himself by name and profession as having been for eighteen years a secret and unaccused prisoner in the Bastille.

He had ascertained that his son-in-law was among the living prisoners, and had pleaded hard to the Tribunal for his life and liberty.

The Doctor also pleaded for permission to remain, and obtained the permission.

The Doctor used his personal influence so wisely that he

was soon the inspecting physician of three prisons, among them La Force.

But, though the Doctor never ceased trying to get Charles Darnay set at liberty, the public current of the time set too strong and fast for him.

Prisons gorged with people who had committed no offence, and could obtain no hearing; these things became the established order and nature of things. Above all, one hideous figure grew familiar – the figure of the sharp female called La Guillotine.

It sheared off heads so many, that it, and the ground it polluted, were a rotten red. It hushed the eloquent, struck down the powerful, abolished the beautiful and good.

Among these terrors, the Doctor walked with a steady head, never doubting that he would save Lucie's husband at last. Yet the current of the time swept time away so fiercely, that Charles had lain in prison one year and three months.

The Wood-sawyer

One year and three months. During all that time Lucie was never sure but that the Guillotine would strike off her husband's head the next day. Every day, through the stony streets, the tumbrils now jolted heavily, filled with Condemned, all red wine for La Guillotine.

Her father said to her, on coming home one evening. "My dear, there is an upper window in the prison, to which Charles can sometimes gain access at three in the afternoon. He might see you in the street, he thinks, if you stood in a certain place."

From that time, in all weathers, she waited there two hours. As the clock struck two, she was there, and at four she turned away. She never missed a single day.

It was the dark corner of a small street. The hovel of a

cutter of wood was the only house. "Walking here again, citizeness?"

"You see me, citizen!"

The wood-sawyer, who had once been a mender of roads, pointed at the prison. "But it's not my business," said he.

Thenceforth, to secure his good will, Lucie always spoke to him first, and often gave him drink-money.

He was an inquisitive fellow, and sometimes when she had forgotten him in gazing at the prison she would find him looking at her. "But it's not my business!" he would say.

These occupations brought her round to the December month, wherein her father walked among the terrors with a steady head. On a lightly snowing afternoon she arrived at the usual corner. Presently she heard a troubled movement and a shouting which filled her with fear. A throng of people came pouring round the corner, in the midst of whom was the wood-sawyer. There could not be fewer than five hundred people, and they were dancing like five thousand demons. There was no other music than their own singing. They danced to the popular Revolution song, keeping a ferocious time that was like a gnashing of teeth. They advanced, retreated, struck at one another's hands, clutched at one another's heads, spun round alone, caught one another and spun round in pairs, until many of them dropped. No fight could have been half so terrible as this dance. This was the Carmagnole.

It passed, leaving Lucie frightened and bewildered.

"O my father!" for he stood before her when she lifted up the eyes she had darkened with her hand; "such a cruel, bad sight."

A footstep in the snow. Madame Defarge. "I salute you, citizeness," from the Doctor.

"I salute you, citizen." This in passing. Nothing more.

Madame Defarge gone.

"Give me your arm, my love. Charles is summoned for tomorrow. He has not received the notice yet, but I know that he will be removed to the Conciergerie. He shall be restored to you within a few hours. I must see Lorry."

It was almost dark when they arrived at the Bank.

Who could that be with Mr Lorry – the owner of the riding-coat upon the chair – who must not be seen? From whom newly arrived, did he come out? To whom, raising his voice and turning his head towards the door of the room from which he had issued, did he say: "Removed to the Conciergerie, and summoned for tomorrow?"

Triumph

The dread Tribunal of five Judges, Public Prosecutor, and determined Jury, sat every day. Their lists went forth every evening, and were read out by the gaolers of the various prisons to their prisoners.

"Charles Evrémonde, called Darnay," was at length arraigned.

Looking at the Jury and the turbulent audience, he might have thought that the usual order of things was reversed, and that the felons were trying the honest men. The lowest, cruellest, and worst populace of a city were the directing spirits of the scene, noisily commenting, applauding, disapproving, without a check. Of the men, the greater part were armed; of the women, some wore knives, some ate and drank, many knitted. Among these last, was one, with a spare piece of knitting under her arm as she worked. She was by the side of a man whom he remembered as Defarge.

Charles Evrémonde, called Darnay, was accused by the public prosecutor as an emigrant, whose life was forfeit to the Republic, under the decree which banished all emigrants on pain of Death. His head was demanded.

"Take off his head!" cried the audience.

The President asked the prisoner whether he had lived many years in England? Was he not an emigrant then? What did he call himself?

Not an emigrant, he hoped, because he had voluntarily relinquished a title that was distasteful to him, and a station that was distasteful to him, and had left his country to live by his own industry in England, rather than on the industry of the overladen people of France.

But he had married in England? Her name and family?

"Lucie Manette, only daughter of Doctor Manette, the good physician who sits there."

This answer had a happy effect upon the audience. Cries in exaltation of the well-known good physician rent the hall.

The President asked, why had he returned to France?

He had returned on the written entreaty of a French citizen, who represented that his life was endangered by his absence. He had come back to save a citizen's life. Was that criminal in the eyes of the Republic?

The populace cried enthusiastically, "No!"

The President required the name of that citizen. The accused explained that the citizen was Gabelle.

Citizen Gabelle was called to confirm it, and did so.

At every vote (the Jurymen voted aloud and individually), the populace set up a shout of applause. All the voices were in the prisoner's favour, and the President declared him free.

A Knock at the Door

One evening a blow struck upon the door of the lodging, and four rough men in red caps, armed with sabres and pistols, entered the room. "The Citizen Evrémonde, called

Darnay," said the first. "You are again the prisoner of the Republic. You return straight to the Conciergerie, and are summoned for tomorrow."

Dr Manette asked, "How does this happen?"

"Citizen Doctor," said the first, "he is accused by Saint Antoine."

"Will you tell me who denounced him?"

"It is against rule. But he is denounced by the Citizen and Citizeness Defarge. And by one other."

"What other?"

"You will be answered tomorrow. Now, I am dumb!"

A Hand at Cards

Happily unconscious of the new calamity at home, Miss Pross crossed the river, reckoning in her mind the number of indispensable purchases she had to make. Mr Cruncher walked at her side. Miss Pross bethought herself of the wine they wanted.

As their wine was measuring out, a man parted and rose to depart. No sooner did he face her, than Miss Pross uttered a scream, and clapped her hands.

"What is the matter?" said the man who had caused Miss Pross to scream; speaking in a vexed, abrupt voice (though in a low tone), and in English.

"Oh, Solomon, dear brother!" cried Miss Pross.

"Don't call me Solomon. Do you want to be the death of me?" asked the man in a frightened way. "Come out, if you want to speak to me."

"Now," said Solomon, stopping at the dark street corner, "if you expect me to be surprised, I am not surprised; I knew you were here; I know of most people who are here. Go your way as soon as possible, and let me go mine. I am busy. I am an official."

Mr Cruncher, interposed with the following singular

question: "I say! Might I ask the favour? As to whether your name is John Solomon, or Solomon John? She calls you Solomon, and she must know, being your sister. And *I* know you're John. And regarding that name of Pross. That warn't your name over the water. You was a spy-witness at the Bailey. What was you called at that time?"

"Barsad," said another voice.

The speaker was Sydney Carton.

"Don't be alarmed," he said. "I arrived at Mr Lorry's yesterday evening; I present myself here to talk with your brother. I wish for you sake he was not a spy of the Prisons. I lighted on you, Mr Barsad, coming out of the prison of the Conciergerie an hour or more ago. I remember faces well. I walked into the wine-shop close after you, and sat near you. I had no difficulty in deducing the nature of your calling. Could you favour me with some minutes of your company – at the office of Tellson's Bank?"

"I'll hear what you have got to say. Yes, I'll go with you."

Mr Lorry turned his head as they entered, and showed the surprise with which he saw a stranger.

"Miss Pross's brother, sir," said Sydney. "Mr Barsad. Witness at that trial."

"Mr Barsad has been recognised by Miss Pross," said Sydney, "and has acknowledged the relationship. I pass to worse news. Darnay has been arrested again. When was it done, Mr Barsad?"

"Just now."

"I am shaken, Mr Lorry, by Doctor Manette's not having had the power to prevent this arrest," said Sydney. "This is a desperate time, when desperate games are played for desperate stakes. The stake I have resolved to play for is a friend in the Conciergerie. And the friend I purpose to myself to win, is Mr Barsad."

"You need have good cards, sir," said the spy.

"I'll see what I hold."

"Mr Barsad, spy and secret informer, represents himself to his employers under a false name. That's a very good card. Mr Barsad, now in the employ of the French was formerly in the employ of the aristocratic English government, the enemy of France. That's an excellent card. Inference clear as day that Mr Barsad is the spy of Pitt, the English traitor and agent of all mischief so much spoken of and so difficult to find. That's a card not to be beaten. I play my Ace, Denunciation of Mr Barsad to the nearest Section Committee. Look over your hand, Mr Barsad, and see what you have."

It was a poor hand. Mr Barsad saw losing cards in it. Thrown out of employment in England, he had crossed the Channel, and accepted service in France: first, as a tempter and an eavesdropper among his own countrymen there: gradually, as a tempter and an eavesdropper among the natives. He knew that under the overthrown government he had been a spy upon Saint Antoine and Defarge's wine-shop.

"I have a strong impression that I have another good card here," said Carton. "That friend and fellow-spy, who was he? Cly! Disguised, but the same man."

"Now you are hasty, sir," said Barsad. "Cly has been dead several years. I helped to lay him in his coffin."

Mr Cruncher rose and stepped forward. "That there Roger Cly, master," he said. "Cly was never in that there coffin. You buried paving-stones and earth in that coffin. Me and two more knows it."

Barsad turned to Sydney Carton. "It has come to a point. I go on duty soon, and can't overstay my time. You told me you had a proposal; what is it?"

"You are a turnkey at the Conciergerie?"

"I can pass in and out when I choose."

"So far, we have spoken before these two," said Carton. "Come into the dark room here, and let us have one final word alone."

The Game Made

Sydney Carton and the spy returned from the dark room. "Adieu, Mr Barsad," said the former.

When they were alone, Mr Lorry asked him what he had done?

"Not much. If it should go ill with the prisoner, I have ensured access to him, once. It is all I could do," said Carton.

Carton left and stopped at a chemist's shop, laying a scrap of paper before him. "Whew!" the chemist whistled softly. "You will be careful to keep them separate, citizen? You know the consequences of mixing them?"

"Perfectly."

Certain small packets were made and given to him.

Next morning the court was all astir and a-buzz when Carton took his place. Mr Lorry was there, and Doctor Manette was there. Lucie was there, sitting beside her father.

Charles Evrémonde, called Darnay. Released yesterday. Reaccused and retaken yesterday. Suspected and denounced enemy of the Republic, one of a family of tyrants, one of a race proscribed.

The President asked, was the Accused openly denounced? By whom?

"Three voices. Ernest Defarge, Thérèse Defarge, his wife, Alexandre Manette, physician."

A great uproar took place in the court, and in the midst of it, Doctor Manette was seen, pale and trembling, standing where he had been seated. "President, I indignantly protest to you that this is a forgery and a fraud."

Defarge was produced, and expounded the story of the imprisonment, and of the release, and of the state of the prisoner when released and delivered to him.

"You did good service at the taking of the Bastille, citizen?"

"I believe so. I knew that this prisoner had been confined in a cell known as One Hundred and Five, North Tower. I resolved to examine that cell. In a hole in the chimney I find a written paper. This is that written paper, the writing of Doctor Manette."

The Substance of the Shadow

"I, Alexandre Manette, unfortunate physician, native of Beauvais, write this in the Bastille, during the last month of the year 1767. One cloudy moonlight night, in the third week of December in the year 1757, I was walking by the Seine when a carriage came along, driven very fast. A head was put out at the window, and a voice called to the driver to stop. The same voice called to me by my name. I answered, and two gentlemen alighted. They were both wrapped in cloaks, and appeared to conceal themselves. As they stood side by side I also observed that they were greatly alike, in stature, manner, voice, and (as far as I could see) face too. Almost like twin brothers.

"'Doctor Manette, formerly of Beauvais, the young physician, originally an expert surgeon, who has a rising reputation in Paris? Will you please to enter the carriage?'

"The carriage stopped at a solitary house. I heard cries proceeding from an upper chamber. I was conducted to this chamber, the cries growing louder as we ascended the stairs, and I found a patient in a high fever of the brain, lying on a bed.

"The patient was a woman of great beauty, and young; assuredly not much past twenty. Her hair was torn and ragged, and her arms were bound to her sides with sashes. On one of them I saw the armorial bearings of a Noble, and the letter E.

"Her eyes were wild, and she constantly uttered piercing shrieks, and repeated the words, 'My husband, my father, and my brother!' and then counted up to twelve, and said, 'Hush!' For an instant, she would pause to listen, and then the piercing shrieks would begin again, and she would repeat the cry.

"'She has a husband, a father, and a brother?' I asked.

"'A brother.'

"'She has some association with the number twelve?'

"'With twelve o'clock.'

"I made the patient swallow some medicine and waited.

"'There is another patient,' said the elder brother.

"The other patient lay in a back room, a handsome peasant-boy of not more than seventeen. The wound was a sword-thrust. He was dying fast.

"'How has this been done, monsieur?' said I to the elder brother.

"'A crazed young common dog! Forced my brother to draw upon him, and has fallen by my brother's sword.'

"The boy's eyes slowly moved to me. 'Doctor, they are very proud, these Nobles; but we common dogs are proud too, sometimes. She – have you seen her, Doctor?'

"I said, 'I have seen her.'

"'She is my sister, Doctor. She was a good girl. We were all tenants of that man who stands there.'

"'Doctor, my sister married. She had not been married many weeks, when that man's brother saw her and admired her, and asked that man to lend her to him. To persuade her husband they harnessed him to a cart and drove him. They kept him out at night, and ordered him back into his harness in the day. But he was not persuaded. No! taken out of harness one day at noon, to feed – if he could find food – he sobbed twelve times, once for every stroke of the bell, and died on her bosom.'

"'Then, with that man's permission his brother took her away. I took my young sister (for I have another) to a place beyond the reach of this man, then I tracked the brother here. Where is the man who was here? Turn my face to him. Marquis,' said the boy, 'in the days when all these things are to be answered for, I summon you and yours, to the last of your bad race, to answer for them.'

"I laid him down dead and when I returned to the bedside of the young woman, I found her raving in precisely the same order and continuity.

"This lasted twenty-six hours when she began to falter, and lay like the dead. It was then that I knew her condition to be that of one in whom the first expectations of being a mother have arisen.

"She lingered for a week. 'At last she is dead?' said the elder.

"'She is dead,' said I. He gave me gold. I took it from his hand, but laid it on the table.

"'Pray excuse me,' said I. 'Under the circumstances, no.' We parted without another word on either side.

"Early in the morning, the gold was left at my door. I decided to write privately to the Minister, stating the nature of the two cases to which I had been summoned. I wished to relieve my own mind. The letter was lying before me just completed, when I was told that a lady wished to see me.

"The lady was the wife of the Marquis St Evrémonde. I connected the title by which the boy had addressed the elder brother, with the initial letter embroidered on the scarf. She had discovered the main facts of the cruel story. She had reasons for believing that there was a young sister living, and her greatest desire was, to help that sister. I could tell her nothing but that there was such a sister; beyond that, I knew nothing. When I handed her down to the door, there was a child, two to three years old, in her carriage.

"'For his sake, Doctor,' she said, 'I would do all I can to make what poor amends I can. He will never prosper in his inheritance otherwise.'

"She kissed the boy, and said, 'It is for thine own dear sake. Thou wilt be faithful, little Charles?' The child answered her bravely, 'Yes!' I never saw her more.

"I sealed my letter and delivered it myself that day.

"That night, the last night of the year, towards nine o'clock, a man in a black dress rang at my gate.

"'An urgent case', he said. He had a coach in waiting.

"When I was clear of the house, a black muffler was drawn over my mouth and my arms were pinioned. The two brothers identified me with a single gesture. The Marquis took from his pocket the letter I had written, burnt it in the light of a lantern and extinguished the ashes with his foot. Not a word was spoken. I was brought here, I was brought to my living grave.

"Them and their descendants, to the last of their race, I, Alexandre Manette, unhappy prisoner, do this last night in the year 1767, denounce to the times when all these things shall be answered for. I denounce them to Heaven and to earth."

A terrible sound arose when the reading of this document was done.

At every juryman's vote, there was a roar. Another and another. Roar and roar.

Unanimously voted. Back to the Conciergerie, and Death within four-and-twenty hours!

Dusk

The tribunal adjourned. Lucie stood stretching out her arms towards her husband. "If I might embrace him once!"

Barsad proposed, "Let her embrace him."

Her father followed her, and would have fallen on his knees, but that Darnay seized him, crying: “No, no! What have you done, that you should kneel to us! We know now, what you underwent when you suspected my descent, and when you knew it. It was the always-vain endeavour to discharge my poor mother's trust that first brought my fatal presence near you. Be comforted, and forgive me. Heaven bless you!”

Sydney Carton came and took her up, carried her lightly to the door, and laid her tenderly down in a coach.

When they arrived he lifted her again, and laid her down on a couch, where her child and Miss Pross wept over her.

“Oh, Carton, Carton, dear Carton!” cried little Lucie. “Now that you have come, I think you will do something to help mamma, something to save papa! Can you, of all people who love her, bear to see her so?”

“Before I go,” he said, and paused – “I may kiss her?”

It was remembered afterwards that he murmured some words. The child, heard him say, “A life you love.”

When he had gone out into the next room, he turned suddenly on Mr Lorry and her father, and said, “You had great influence yesterday, Doctor Manette; let it at least be tried. The hours between this and tomorrow afternoon are few and short, but try.”

“I intend to try. I will not rest a moment.”

“It will be dark soon after four. If I go to Mr Lorry's at nine, shall I hear what you have done?”

“Yes.”

Darkness

Sydney Carton paused in the street, and turned towards Saint Antoine.

He went direct to Defarge's, and went in.

There happened to be no customer in the shop but Jacques Three, in conversation with the Defarges.

Carton walked in, took his seat and asked (in very indifferent French) for a small measure of wine.

"English?" asked Madame Defarge.

"Yes, madame, yes. I am English!"

Madame Defarge returned to her counter and he heard her say, "I swear to you, like Evrémonde!"

After a silence of a few moments, during which they all looked towards him, they resumed their conversation.

"It is true what madame says," observed Jacques Three. "Why stop?"

"Well, well," reasoned Defarge, "but one must stop somewhere."

"At extermination," said madame.

"Extermination is good doctrine," said Defarge. "But this Doctor has suffered much; you observed his face when the paper was read."

"I have observed his face!" repeated madame. "I have observed his face to be not the face of a true friend of the Republic! For other crimes as tyrants and oppressors, I have this race a long time on my register, doomed to destruction and extermination. That peasant family so injured by the two Evrémonde brothers, is my family, that sister of the mortally wounded boy was my sister, that husband was my sister's husband, that unborn child was their child, that brother was my brother, that father was my father, those dead are my dead, and that summons to answer for those things descends to me!"

Customers entered, and the group was broken up. The English customer asked to be directed towards the National Palace.

He was soon swallowed up in the shadow of the prison

wall. At the appointed hour, he presented himself in Mr Lorry's room again.

The instant Doctor Manette entered the room, it was plain that all was lost. They asked him no question, for his face told them everything.

"Where is my bench?" he said. "What have they done with my work? Time presses: I must finish those shoes."

They looked at one another, and their hearts died within them. Lost utterly lost!

Carton was the first to speak: "The last chance is gone; he had better be taken to her. But, before you go, will you, steadily attend to me? Don't ask me why I exact the promise I am going to exact; I have a reason – a good one."

"I don't doubt it," answered Mr Lorry. "Say on."

"First," he put his hand in his coat, and took a paper from it, "that is the certificate which enables me to pass out of this city. Keep it for me, and this similar certificate, enabling Doctor Manette and his daughter and her child, to pass the barrier and the frontier. "They are in great danger. They are in danger of denunciation by Madame Defarge. I have seen the spy. He confirms me. This new denunciation will not take place until after tomorrow. Buy the means of travelling to the coast as quickly as the journey can be made. Early tomorrow have your horses ready, so that they may start at two o'clock in the afternoon. Have all these arrangements made in the court-yard here, even to the taking of your own seat in the carriage. The moment I come to you, take me in, and drive away. Wait for nothing but to have my place occupied, and then for England! Now goodbye!"

The Exchange

In the black prison of the Conciergerie, the doomed of the

day awaited their fate.

The hours went on and the clocks struck the numbers Darnay would never hear again. Nine gone for ever, ten gone for ever, eleven gone for ever, twelve gone for ever. The final hour was Three, and he knew he would be summoned earlier, as the tumbrils jolted heavily and slowly through the streets.

One struck. "There is but another now," he said.

Footsteps in the stone passage outside. He stopped.

The key was put in the lock, and turned. Before the door was opened, a man said in English: "He has never seen me here. Go in alone; I wait near. Lose no time!"

The door was opened and closed, and there stood Sydney Carton.

"I am possessed of a power over one of the keepers here, and in virtue of it I stand before you. I come from your wife, dear Darnay," said Carton. "I bring you a request from her. You must comply with it – take off those boots you wear, and draw on these of mine."

"Carton, there is no escaping from this place; it never can be done. You will only die with me. It is madness."

"It would be madness if I asked you to escape; but do I? Change that cravat for this of mine, that coat for this of mine. While you do it, let me take this ribbon from your hair, and shake out your hair like this of mine!"

"Write what I shall dictate. Quick, friend, quick! 'If you remember,'" said Carton, dictating, "'the words that passed between us, long ago, you will readily comprehend this when you see it.'"

He was drawing his hand from his breast; the prisoner saw it. "Is that a weapon in your hand?" he asked.

"No. Write on. 'I am thankful that the time has come, when I can prove them.'" As he said these words his hand slowly moved down close to the writer's face.

The pen dropped from Darnay's fingers on the table, and he looked about him vacantly.

"What vapour is that?" he asked.

For a few seconds he faintly struggled with the man who had come to lay down his life for him; but, within a minute he was stretched insensible on the ground.

Quickly Carton dressed himself in the clothes the prisoner had laid aside. Then he called, "Come in!" and the Spy presented himself.

"Take him to the coach," said Carton. "Say that I was weak and faint when you brought me in, and I am fainter now you take me out. The parting interview has overpowered me. Quick!"

The door closed, and Carton was left alone. He listened for any sound that might denote suspicion or alarm. There was none. Breathing more freely in a little while, he sat down at the table, and listened again until the clock struck Two.

Several doors were opened in succession, and finally his own. A gaoler looked in, merely saying, "Follow me, Evrémonde!" and he followed into a large dark room, where others were brought to have their arms bound. The majority were silent and still, looking fixedly at the ground.

The same shadows that are falling on the prison, are falling, in that same hour of the early afternoon, on the Barrier when a coach going out of Paris drives up to be examined.

"Who goes here? Papers!" The papers are handed out, and read. "Alexandre Manette. Physician. Lucie. His daughter. Lucie, her child. Sydney Carton. Advocate. English. Which is he?"

He lies in the corner of the carriage. He is pointed out.

"Jarvis Lorry. Banker. English. Which is he?"

"I am he."

"Behold your papers, Jarvis Lorry, countersigned.

Forward! A good journey!"

"I salute you, citizens. And the first danger passed!"

The Knitting Done

Madame Defarge held darkly ominous council with Jacques Three of the Revolutionary Jury.

"Defarge," said Jacques Three, "is undoubtedly a good Republican? Eh?"

"My husband, fellow-citizen, is a good Republican and a bold man. But my husband has his weaknesses, and he is so weak as to relent towards this Doctor. But, the Evrémonde people are to be exterminated, and the wife and child must follow the husband and father. My husband has not my reason for pursuing this family to annihilation. I must act for myself, therefore. She will now be at home, awaiting the moment of his death. She will be mourning and grieving. She will be in a state of mind to impeach the justice of the Republic. I will go to her."

When the journey had been planned last night, the difficulty of taking Miss Pross in it had much engaged Mr Lorry's attention. It was not merely desirable to avoid overloading the coach, but it was of the highest importance that the time occupied in examining its passengers, should be reduced to the utmost. Finally, he had proposed that Miss Pross and Jerry, who were at liberty to leave the city, should leave at three o'clock in the lightest-wheeled conveyance. They would soon overtake the coach, and, would greatly facilitate its progress during the precious hours of the night.

Miss Pross and Jerry were concluding their arrangements to follow the coach as Madame Defarge drew nearer.

"Take me in to the carriage near the great cathedral door between the two towers at three o'clock," said Miss Pross, and Mr Cruncher went out and left her by herself to follow as she had proposed.

She looked at her watch, and it was twenty minutes past two. She had no time to lose. Miss Pross got a basin of cold water and began laving her eyes, which were swollen and red, but constantly paused and looked round to see that there was no one watching her. In one of those pauses she cried out, for she saw a figure standing in the room.

Madame Defarge said, "The wife of Evrémonde; where is she?"

Miss Pross placed herself before the door of the chamber which Lucie had occupied.

Madame Defarge raised her voice and called out, "Citizen Doctor! Wife of Evrémonde! Child of Evrémonde! Any person answer the Citizeness Defarge!"

Perhaps the following silence whispered to Madame Defarge that they were gone. Three doors she opened swiftly, and looked in.

"I will have you from that door," said Madame Defarge, and made at the door.

Miss Pross seized her round the waist in both her arms, and held her tight.

Madame Defarge's hands were at her bosom. Miss Pross saw the loaded pistol, struck at it, struck out a flash and a crash, and stood alone.

All this was in a second. Madame Defarge's body lay lifeless on the ground.

Miss Pross arrived at the cathedral, where the escort took her in, and took her away.

The Footsteps Die Out For Ever

Along the Paris streets, the death-carts rumble, hollow and harsh. Six tumbrils carry the day's wine to La Guillotine.

The clocks are on the stroke of three. In front of the

Guillotine, seated in chairs, are a number of women, busily knitting.

"Thérèse!" cries one. "Who has seen her? Thérèse Defarge!"

"She never missed before," says another. "Evrémonde will be despatched in a wink, and she not here!"

The tumbrils begin to discharge their loads. Crash! A head is held up, and the knitting-women count One.

The supposed Evrémonde descends – is gone. Twenty-three.

* * *

They said of him, about the city that night, that it was the peacefullest man's face ever beheld there. Many added that he looked prophetic.

One of the most remarkable sufferers by the same axe – a woman – had asked at the foot of the same scaffold, not long before, to be allowed to write down the thoughts that were inspiring her. If he had given an utterance to his, and they were prophetic, they would have been these:

"I see Barsad, and Cly, Defarge, the Juryman, long ranks of the new oppressors who have risen on the destruction of the old, perishing by this instrument, before it shall cease out of its present use. I see a beautiful city and a brilliant people rising from this abyss. I see the evil of this time gradually making expiation for itself and wearing out.

"I see the lives for which I lay down my life, peaceful, useful, prosperous and happy, in that England which I shall see no more.

"I see that I hold a sanctuary in their hearts, and in the hearts of their descendants, generations hence. I see Lucie, an old woman, weeping for me on the anniversary of this day.

"It is a far, far better thing that I do, than I have ever done; it is a far, far better rest that I go to than I have ever known."